Also by Elizabeth Daly
in Thorndike Large Print

Unexpected Night